Visit from
an Angel

Teddy E. Assiter

Carpenter's Son Publishing

Visit from an Angel
©2023 Teddy E. Assiter

Cover and Interior Design by Suzanne Lawing

978-1-956370-10-2

Printed in the United States of America

FORWARD

Our relationship with Ted Assiter began some twenty-three years ago in a prison in Lubbock, Texas. Neither of us were in prison but working at a Karios Ministry together. During this time, he started dating his soon to be wife, Corky Fullingim. We had lost all but one of our parents and they decided we needed to be adopted. We have never met a man with such patriotism and integrity all bundled up as in Ted. His love for God has been amazing to watch. His generosity, along with Corky has been a blessing for our family. Whether it was sharing their mountain home or biscuits and sausage gravy on Saturday morning at their home in Lubbock. Ted Assiter is a man's man, he is not afraid to lead you to Christ, not afraid to show emotions, and still USMC strong very day and was proud to serve our great nation. And with all these great attributes he can play a pretty mean game of poker. Our life was made better by having this wonderful relationship and those days we struggle to understand what's God plan for our Iife.

All I have to do is watch and learn from our great friend, stepdad, and mentor Teddy Assiter.

In Christ's love,
Jim-Tonja Richardson

Chapter 1

Johnson was no ordinary angel! My first thought was that he had lost his driver license when he rode up on his bicycle early that morning on May 8th.

Had he been a victim of DWI? Had he lost his license as a result of a vehicle accident? It was unusual to see a middle-aged man pedal his bicycle with full packs on his back ready to ship out. His clothes were layered three or four deep. On his back was a full pack with a roll tied underneath, and a side pack under each arm.

His appearance was shabby, his clothes dirty, and he hadn't had a bath in awhile. Yet, you could sense this individual was in excellent health and physical shape. His face was tanned and rough looking from the elements of the weather.

Little did I realize at this time that he carried all his worldly possessions on his bike and in packs. My second thought was he was a roost-about or wonderer. Then I realized this was my first encounter with a homeless person. Mayb he was just on the move. I wasn't sure. Do you ask a person if they are homeless? How does one find out?

Chapter 2

The way it all started is clear in my mind as it was only yesterday. Rafael and Cheryl lived next door to us and were getting ready to have an evening graduation party for Rafael's son, Michael, who was about to graduate from nursing school. The year before they had a graduation party for Rafael's son, Robert. He graduated from law school.

Cheryl was a schoolteacher and had limited time to work in flower beds to prepare for the event; plus, the fence was about to fall. Another good west Texas breeze and they might not have a fence! Rafeal was a physician, with no fence-building skills. Cheryl had received a quote from a fence company to install a new fence, including the common fence between our properties. I was consulted about my share of this new fence.

I had retired the previous year. After seeing the fence company quote, I realized I could build us a better fence for less money. They hired me to build the fence with my superb fence design for the same price on condition it had to be finished before the graduation party! No problem, I thought, as I had several weeks to accomplish this task.

Diggin post holes gave me blisters, so I called the state employment agency to send out day-laborers to help me with the project. As we replaced the fence, Cheryl replaced flowers in the flower beds. Cheryl had me get day labor for her to dig or whatever she needed done in the backyard while I was installing the fence.

Chapter 3

The next time I heard from Johnson was Thursday May 30th. My wife came to my workshop and told me I had a collect call from him. I accepted the call and Johnson told me he needed prayer. While he and I built the fence, we had several discussions about salvation, the Bible, masons (?) and church. He said he was in Gordon, Texas headed for Lubbock and was there work available? Rose across the street had said she needed some work done and Cheryl still needed work done, and I could use some day-labor to paint the house trim and garage doors, and pull nails out of boards.

On Sunday June 1st, Johnson called to telling he had made it to Lubbock, and would be out to work the next morning. He asked if I could put on a pot of coffee around 6:30 am. I told him I would; then he asked if I had a piece of bacon left over; I asked if he'd like a couple of eggs with it? "That would be nice", he said.

It was good to see Johnson again as we had breakfast Monday morning. I had missed him since our fence building days. He ask what I had done about the Samaritan Order? In the early 1980's when I wrote the Samaritan Order, and the first five lessons, it was my dream to establish the order for the Glory of Jesus. The time did not seem right, and those people I talked with about the order were not interested in developing the order. With so many "nos"and "not interested" the manual returned time and time again to my desk drawer or filing cabinet. The purpose of writing the order was to fulfill a dream. Always leave home on a Monday morning and return on Friday. During the week in state after state, town after town, and one motel after another; I wished to create a way where we road warriors could develop friendships, recognize each other and serve and witness for Jesus.

I told Johnson nothing had been done since the last time we had discussed it. "Then you can't follow you own advice," Johnson told me. "What advice is that?" l asked. "You don't remember this piece of paper you give me?" as he handed it to me. As I unfolded the paper I began to read "When things go wrong, as they sometimes will, When the road you're trudging seems all uphill. When the funds are low, and the debts are high. And you want to smile, but you have to sign. When care is pressing you down a bit, rest if you must, but don't quit. Life is strange with its twists and turns, as everyone of us sometimes learns, and many a failure turns about. When he might have won had he stuck it out; don't give up though the pace seem slow, you may succeed with another blow. Success is failure turned inside out, The silver tint of the clouds of doubt; and you can never tell how close you are, it may be near when it seems far; so stick to the fight when you're hardest hit. It's when things seem worst you must not quit". I handed the paper back to Johnson. "Do you remember what you told me about mason?" Johnson ask. We had several discussions while we were fence building. "Do you remember saying the master degree (third degree) is the highest?" I had told Johnson that after the master mason degree that all other degrees were honorary. That a thirty-second degree was no higher than the third degree. It was like two men came to this country, and after the requirement; were met they each became a citizens. One citizen had wealth so he visited Grand Canyon, Yellowstone Park, Statue of Liberty, Mount Rushmore and other places. He was no more a citizen of this country than the other man; but had seen more of what he was a citizen. I got Johnson the paint and ladder and he started painting the house trim.

Chapter 4

All the work in the neighbor had been finished and Johnson told me he thought he would go to Odessa where the oil field were needing a larger work force and jobs were plentiful. As he started to leave he asked if I wanted to see his new Bible? "Sure" I said. And Johnson took a deck of cards from his pocket. "Here is a new way to look at a deck of cards. You see the ace? It reminds me that there is only one God. The two represents the two parts of the Bible, Old and New Testaments. The three represents the Father, Son, and the Holy Ghost. The four stands for the four gospels: Matthew, Mark, Luke and John. The five is for the five virgin. There were ten, but only five of them were glorified. The six is for six days it took God to create the Heavens and Earth. The seven is for the day God rested after making His Creation. The eight is for the family of Noah and his wife, their three sons and their wives (the eight people God spared from the flood that destroyed the Earth. The nine is for the lepers that Jesus cleansed of leprosy. He cleansed ten, but nine never thanked Him. The ten represents the Ten Commandments that God handed down to Moses on tablets made of stone. The jack is a reminder of Satan, one of God's first angels, but he got kicked out of heaven for his sly and wicked ways and is now the joker of eternal hell. The queen stands for the virgin Mary. The king stands for Jesus for He is the King of all kings. When I count the dots on all the cards, I come up with 365 total, one for every day of the year. There are a total of 52 cards in a deck: each is a week (52 weeks in a year). The four suits represent the our seasons: spring, summer, fall, and winter. Each suit has thirteen cards (there are exactly thirteen weeks in a quarter. So when I want to talk to God and thank Him, I just pull out this deck of cards and they remind me of all that I have to be thankful for." The Bible tells us that angels walk among us. One time when Johnson and I were talking about holidays I got a laugh when he thought Thanksgiving Day began with some Indians and pilgrims at Plymouth Rock. He didn't know it was by the President of the United State of America: A Proclamation [note semi-legible, "not all capital] "... We have been the recipients of the choicest bounties of heaven. We have grown in numbers, wealth and power as no ther nation has ever grown. But we have forgotten God. We have forgotten the gracious hand which preserved us in peace, and multiplied and enriched and strengthened us, and we have vainly imagined in the deceitfulness of our hearts that all these blessings were produced by [?] some superior wisdom and virtue of our own. Intoxicated with unbroken success, we have become too self-sufficient to feel the necessity of redeeming and preserving grace – too proud to pray to the God that had made us. It has seemed to me fit and proper that God should be solemnly, reverently, and gratefully acknowledged as with one heart and one voice by the whole American people. I do, therefore, invite my fellow citizens in every part of the United States and also those at sea and those who are sojourning in foreign lands, to set apart and observe the last Thursday of November next, as a day of Thanksgiving and Praise to our benevolent Father who dwelleth in the Heavens." Abraham Lincoln, October 3, 1863

How can you tell if you have been in contact with an angel? The Bible tells us in Psalms 91:11-12 (KJV) "For he shall give his angels charge over thee in all thy ways. They shall bear thee up in their hands, lest thou doth dash thy foot against a stone." And from Genesis thru Revelation I read where angels are everywhere fulfilling the desires of God. It tells where Satan changed into an "angel of light" and was no other than Lucifer who was cast out from Heaven.

Johnson was right about me quitting on creating the Samaritan Order. I submit the manual to you to get your opinion.

Samaritan

In the early 1980's when I wrote the Samaritan Order, and the first five lessons, it was my dream to establish the order for the Glory of Jesus. The time did not seem right, and those people I talked with about the order were not interested in developing the order. With so many "nos" and "not interested" the manual returned time and time again to my desk drawer or filing cabinet.

The purpose of writing the order was to fulfill a dream. Most of my life was spent as a representative for one company or another. Always leaving home on each Monday morning to return on Friday. During the week in state after state, town after town; and motel after another: I wished to create a way where we road warriors could develop friendships, recognize each other and service and witness for Jesus.

In the almost twenty years, since I wrote the order and first five lessons, It appears to me Christ is being left out of so many families. That, now is the time to establish the Samaritan Order, and hope we can somehow make a difference. If we Samaritans witness and bring one lost person to accept Jesus as his savior, then all the work will be well worthwhile. Plus, maybe we can set a standard in caring, sharing and giving for others to follow in our footsteps, all for the glory of God's Household.

Chapter 5

Petition for Membership

Samaritan Order

TO THE DEACONS OF SAMARITAN ORDER NUMBER

_____

Mr./Miss/Mrs.: _____

REQUESTS TO BECOME A BROTHER/SISTER
OF THIS ORDER

Address: _____

City/State: _____   Zip: _____

Phone: (   ) _____

Employer: _____

Address: _____

City/State: _____

Phone: (   ) _____

Position: _____

Duties: _____

Lesson One Fee...$25.00

Annual Dues..$15.00

$40.00

Do you believe the Holy Bible to be the true word of God?
_____

Do you believe everything the Bible says to be the true truth?
_____

Is it your desire to become a disciple of Jesus, Our Lord, Son to the Most High, and serve the Trinity? _____

Signature: _____

On my honor I will surrender my membership card to the order from which it was issued upon request in writing.

Signature: _____

Membership Number: _____

Officers

THE DEACONS:

Stephen (presiding officer)

Philip (presiding when Stephen is absent)

Proch-o-rus

Ni-ca-nor

Timon

Par-me–nas

Nicotas

The deacons are elected each year from the membership in January. The seven deacons elect Stephen and Philip from their group. The five remaining deacon officers name come from a drawing.

The deacons appoint the secretary.

The deacons elect the elder/elders (no more than three)

Stephen is the only person to wear a hat during the meetings.

The seating of the deacons is as follows:

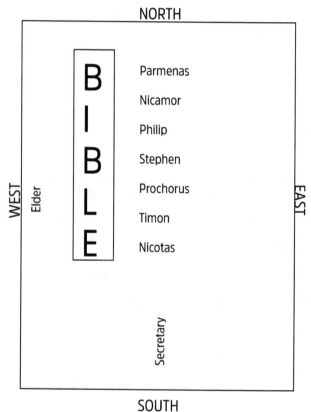

The Holy Bible on the table in front of the deacons is facing Stephen.

OPENING OF THE ORDER

The deacons, elder and secretary take their position in the Order.

Stephen   (Goes to the Holy Bible; opens it to Luke 10. He removes his hat, holding it over his heart he has silent prayer. When his prayer is finished he places his hat on his head, looks toward the brethern and says, "Peace be to this house.") Returns to his seat.

Nicotas   (Goes to Holy Bible, picks it up and reads Luke 10: 1-5. Replaces Holy Bible, and returns to his seat.)

Parmenas   Goes to Holy Bible, picks it up and reads Luke 10: 6-10. Replaces Holy Bible, and returns to his seat.)

Timon   (Goes to Holy Bible, picks it up and reads Luke 10: 11-15. Replaces Holy Bible, and returns to his seat.)

Nicanor   (Goes to Holy Bible, picks it up and reads Luke 10: 16-20. Replaces Holy Bible, and returns to his seat.)

Prochorus   (Goes to Holy Bible, picks it up and reads Luke 10: 21-25. Replaces Holy Bible, and returns to his seat.)

Philip   (Goes to Holy Bible, picks it up and reads Luke 10: 26-30. Stephen joins Philip at the tablei Philip hands the Holy Bible to Stephen, then returns to his seat.)

Stephen	(Removes his hat; reads Luke 10: 31-36. Replaces his hat on his head.) "And he said, he that shewed mercy on him. Then said Jesus unto him.11
All Brethern	In Unison "Go, and do thou likewise."
Stephen	(Returns the Holy Bible to the table, then returns to his seat.)
Stephen	"Brother Secretary."
Secretary	(Stands) "Brother Stephen."
Stephen	"You will pass out the agenda for this meeting to the brotherhood."
Secretary	(Distributes agenda. The deacons receive their copy last; Stands in front of Stephen.) "Brother Stephen the agenda for this meeting has been distributed to the brethen."(Returns to his seat.)
Stephen	"The first order of business is..... "The second order of business is..... "The third order of business is..... ect.
Stephen	"Is there any other business to be conducted at this meeting?" (If no response.) "Then we shaall close this meeting." "Brother Nicotas"
Nicotas	(Places bread and wine on the table; returns to his seat and remains standing.) "God spoke to Moses."

Parmenas (Stands) "You shall have no other gods before me."

Timon (Stands) "You shall not make for yourself a graven image, or any likeness of anything that is in heaven above, or that is in the earth beneath, or that is in the water under the earth; You shall not bow down to them or serve them."

Nicanor (Stands) "You shall not take the name of the Lord your God in vain."

Prochorus "Remember the sabbath day, to keep it holy."

Nicotas "Honor your father and your mother."

Parmenas "You shall not kill.11

Timon "You shall not commit adultery."

Nicanor "You shall not steal.11

Prochorus "You shall not bear false witness against your neighbor."

Nicotas "You shall not covet your neighbor's wife, or anything that is your neighbor's."

Philip (Stands) "Our Lord Jesus said: 'You shall love the Lord your God with all your heart, and with all your soul, and with all your mind. This is the great and first commandment. And a second is like it. You shall love your neighbor as yourself. On these two commandments depend all the law and the prophets."

Stephen (Stands) "As a Samaritan we believe in one God, we believe in one God, the Father, the Almighty, maker of heaven and earth, of all that is seen and unseen. We believe in one Lord, Jesus, the Christ, the only Son of God, eternally begotten of the Father. God from God, Light from Light, true God from true God, begotten, not made, one in Being with the Father. Through Him all things were made. For us men and women, and for our salvation He came down from heaven: by the power of the Holy Spirit He was born 6E the Virgin Mary, and became man. For our sake He was crucified under Pontius Pilate; He suffered, died, and was buried. On the third day He rose again in fulfillment of the Scriptures; He ascended into heaven and is seated at the right hand of the Father. He will come again in glory to judge the living --and the dead, and His kingdom will have no end. We believe in the Holy Spirit, the Lord, the giver of life, who proceeds from the Father and the Son. With the Father and the Son He i.s worshiped and glorified. He has spoken through the prophets. We believe there is only one true church of God; and Jesus is its founding, guarding, sustaining, directing Head.

All Brether   In Unison "AMEN"

Stephen   (Goes to the Holy Bible and removes his hat. He closes the Holy Bible, replaces his hat to his head.) "Brethren! Join me at the table. (All brethren join around the table.)

Stephen   "--And as they were eating Jesus took bread, and blessed it, and brake it, and gave it to the disciples and said; take, eat, this is my body. --And he took the cup, and gave thanks, and give it to them saying: Drink ye all of it; for this is my blood of the new testament, which is shed for many for the remission of sins. But I say unto you. I will not drink henceforth of this fruit of the vine, until that day when I drink it new with you in my Father's kingdom."

(Everyone joins hands in a circle.)

Everyone Sings Together Blest be the tie that binds
Our hearts in Christian love;
The fellowship of kindred minds
Is like the above.

Before our Father's throne,
We pour our ardent prayers;
Our fears, our hopes, our sins are one,
Our comforts and our cares.

We share our mutual woes,
Our mutual burdens bear;
And often for each other flows
The sympathizing tear.

When we asunder part,
It gives us inward pain;
But we shall still be joined in heart
And hope to meet again.

Stephen (At close of hymn) AMEN!

All Members (A slight squeeze of the hands closes the meeting.)

FIRST LESSON RITUAL

The deacons, elder and secretary take their position in the Order.

Stephen   "Honorable Elder?

Elder   "Yes, Brother Stepehen."

Stephen   "Does anyone seek membership in our order?"

Elder   "Yes!" (Then names all candidates.)

Stephen   "Bring all candidates (the candidate) to me that I may ask the questions – to assure the brotherhood they (He/She) believes as we Samaritans."

Elder   (Goes and returns with candidates (canidates) who are blindfolded, and a rope around their (his/her) neck.) The candidate (candiates) is guided in a clockwise circle in the room (symbolic as when Moses led the Children of Israel from Egypt.)

As the circle is walked, the deacons say...

Prochorus   "remember this day, in which ye came out from Egypt, for by strength of hand the Lord brought you from this place."

Nicanor   "And Moses took the bones of Joseph with him; for he had straitly sworn the children of Israel saying, God will surely visit you: And ye shall carry my bones away hence with you."

Timon   "And the Lord went before them, by day in a pillar of a cloud; to lead them they: And by night in a pillar of fire, to give them light."

Nicotas   "The Lord is my strength and song, and he is my salvation."

Elder	(Stops, with candidates (candidate) in front of Stephen.)
Elder	"Honorable deacons, I present to you (names all candidates."
Stephen	(Stands) "Brother Phillip, you will place the candidates left hand upon the Holy Bible."
Philip	(Goes and places the candidates left hand upon the Holy Bible."
Stephen	(Calling candidate (candidates) by name.
	"...You will raise your right arm and hand to the oath position."
	(Philip and Elder make sure the candidates (candidate) are in correct form to answer Stephen's questions.)
	"Do you believe the Holy Bible to be the true word of God?"
Candidate	"I do."
Stephen	"Do you believe everything the Bible says to be the true truth?"
Candidate	"I do."
Stephen	"Is it your desire to become a disciple of Jesus, our Lord, Son of the Most High, and serve the Trinity"?
Candidate	"I do."
Stephen	"Do you further promise, on your honor, to abide by all the laws, and regulations of the order in effect now, or may be enacted in the future as

long as you carry an active membership card?"

Candidate   "I do."

Stephen   "Brother Philip, release (name each candidate) from the blindfold and rope: They are bound to our order by a stronger tie."

(Blindfold and rope is removed from the candidate)

"Being among us – what do you desire?"

Candidate   "A lesson in truth." (Elder Whispers answer to them.)

Stephen   "Then true truth you shall receive. Follow the Elder and he will prepare you for your trip from Jerusalem to Jericho." (They exit room. Philip returns to his seat.

-THE SCENE-

All preparation is made for the ritual; roles are assigned.

Elder   Gives three knocks on the door – then enters with a candidate, goes and stands center North. Watches.

Traveler   Walking from West toward the East. 9may adlib role)

Thieves   (From hiding they ambush him.)

Thief 1   Takes Money (may adlib')

Thief 2   Takes clothes (may adlib')

Thief 3   Wounds him with a knife (may adlib) All thieves depart.

Priest	Walking from East toward the West. – Looks at wounded man and passes on other side (may adlib)
Levite	Walking from West toward the East. – Comes and looks on wounded man, and passes on other side. (may adlib)
	The Elder and candidate make half-circle counterclockwise and and come upon travler. (Elder may adlib)
	(They bandage his wounds.)
	(They cloth him.)
Elder	"What is your name?"
Traveler	(May adlib) Only able to wisper. Finally the traveler whispers the name "Sam A." into the ear of the candidate. A drink is given the traveler. He clears his throat, and speaks "What is your name?"
Candidate	(Elder gives name to candidate, so he can answer: "I. Tan"
	Traveler is carried to an inn (by Elder and candidate) East, behind the table he is laid on pallet on floor.
Elder	"Have you heard the good news? He has risen!!!
Members	"Lights are dimed out one minute) Voice individually "Al-le-lu-ia" (Light are turned up.)
Candidate	(Furnished by the Elder) Gives two pence to the innkeeper.

Elder   "Take care of him and whatsoever thou spendest more, when I come again, I will repay thee."

Elder and Candidate exits.

CHARGE OF LESSON ONE

All candidates who received lesson one are seated in chairs in front of the deacons.

Stephen   "Brother (Sister)" names each; "Ye are now Samaritans!!! "Brother (Sister) what are your thoughts on the lesson you have received?"

Brother
Sister   "----------" answers.

Stephen   Question is repeated until all new brothers (sisters) have given their response.

Stephen   (Stands) "The dramatization in which you took part is recorded in the tenth chapter of the Gospel according to Saint Luke; verses thirty thru thirty-seven of the King James Version of The Holy Bible. As you lived the Good Samaritan act you are taught the foundation of our order: That you are to always give aid and help to those in need --as you are capable of doing --and most important to witness for Jesus at every opportunity."

"The sign of this lesson is this (gives sign) --the left hand extended, palm down; and the right arm and hand in the oath position. --this is your position when you bond yourself to our order; and was released from bondage."

"The passwords of this lesson are the names of the traveler and the Samaritan. The passwords are communicated only in the following manner: When a brother (sister) asks "What is you Samaritan name?" You whisper Sam A to their ear then you ask, "What is your name?" Their response should be, I.Tan. You may remember these words easily if you will observe the emblem of our order. The left horzinal (turns out lights on the rest of the emblen). (Turns all lights back on.) --And the right horzinal (turns out the lights on the rest of the emblem) of our emblem." (Turns all lights back on.)

"It is my pleasure to present to you your weapons to defeat the evil ones."

Stephen   "The Holy Bible, and the Cross.'

The Holy Bible you are to read daily and pray:

This Book of Books should be the rule and guide to your faith and life."

"The cross should always remind you of Jeses – and His blood that gave you salvation. Your cross should be placed in a front window of your home, or in a motel window when traveling, or in a front window of the home where you are a guest; to show your willingness to witness for Jesus at all times."

Nicotas   (Stands) "Ye are the light of the world. A city that is set on a hill cannot be hid." (Sats down.)

Parmenas   (Stands) "-- Neither do men light a candle, and put it under a bushel, but on a candlestick; and it giveth light unto all that are in the house."

(Sats down.)

Timon   (Stands) "-- Let your light so shine before men, that they may see your good world; and glorify your Father which is in heaven." (Sats down.)

Nicanor   (Stands) "Let no man despise thy youth; but be thou an example of the believers, in word, in conversation, in spirit, in faith, in purity. Till I come, give attendance to reading, to exhortation, to doctrine." (Sats down.)

Prochorus   Neglect not the gift that is in thee, which was given thee by prophecy, with the laying on of the hands of the presbytery. Meditate upon these things; give thyself wholly to them; that thy profiting may appear to all. Take heed unto thyself, and unto the doctrine; continue in them; for ib doing this thou shalt both save thyself, and them that hear thee." (Sats down.)

Philip   (Stands) "You will be furnished a decal of the order to be displayed on the rear window of your automobile. On the bottom to your cross is your brotherhood number: The first letters signify the state your order is chartered under: The second letters signify the place of your order: The third letters signify your number in that order: and; the last letters are the date you became a Samaritan. You will be furnished a directory of all Samaritans and revisions monthly. --Therefor; when you see another Samaritan cross, write down the number; go to your directory and you will learn that Samaritan's name, address and vocation. Therefor, you may communicate." (Sats down.)

Stephen   "This Concludes this lesson: You may be seated within the order."

All Brethern In Unison   "AMEN"

SECOND LESSON RITUAL

The deacons, elder and secretary take their position in the order.

Stephen   "Honorable Elder?"

Elder   "Yes, Brother Stephen."

Stephen   "Does anyone seek the lessons of our order?"

Elder   "Yes." (Then names the Brother or Sister) _____ seeks the truth of lesson two. _____ (number)

Stephen   "Bring all brothers (sisters) that seek the truth of lesson two to me."

                Elder goes and returns with those who will receive lesson two. Stands in front of the deacons.

Stephen   (Stands) "Being among us, what do you desire?"

Brother/Sister   "A lesson in truth." (Elder gives the correct answer)

Stephen   "Then truth you shall receive; follow your elder and he will prepare you for lesson two from The Holy Bible," (They exit room)

                All preparation is made for the ritual; roles are assigned.

Stephen	(Goes into the antiroom where the lesson candidate has his (her) back to the door leading into the scene room. The Elder is the guide.)
Stephen	"And there was war in heaven; Michael and his angels fought against the dragon; and the dragon fought and his angels and prevailed not; neither was their place found any more in heaven. And the great dragon was cast out, that old serpent, called the Devil, and Satan, which deceiveth the whole world; he was cast out unto the earth, and his angels were cast out with him." (May adlib'. "Get out of here you wicked ones!!!" (Elder takes candidate thru door.)
Philip	(As Elder and candidate enter they to to North center) Lights are dimmed. "How art thou fallen from heaven, O Lucifer, Son of the morning! how art thou cut down to the ground."

Lights are brighten in the area where Adam is lying.

-THE SCENE-

Adam	(May adlib'.) Lying on the ground in the Garden of Eden. Awakes from sleep; looks around and shows how great everything is that the Lord has made.)
Voice	"Of every tree of the garden, thou mayest freely eat; (Adam reaches for fruit from the tree of knowledge) But NOT OF THAT TREE!!!" (Adam draws hand back) "That is the tree of the knowledge of good and evil, thou shalt not eat of it; for in the day that thou eatest there of·thou shalt surely die."
Adam	(Began to appear bored –nothing to do, sats

and day-dreams.)

Voice   "It is not good that the man should be alone; I will make him an help-mate for him."

(Eve has been under a floor colored sheet all the time at the edge of the scene)

Adam   (May adlib'. Animals are carried to Adam as he names each) He falls asleep near where Eve rests. The sheet is removed from Eve. Awakes, sees Eve. "This is now bone of my bones, and flesh of my flesh; (looks to Eve) You are most beautiful of all. I will call you woman, because you was taken out of man." (Adam showa Eve around the garden, what he has names the an-amials --and near the tree of knowledge·(acts out, they cannot eat of that fruit, points up, makes sign they would die.)

Voice   "Therefore shall a man leave his father and his mother, and shall cleave into his wife: And they shall.be one flesh." (Adam goes away and Eve is alone. Elder and candidate go near her. She is not afraid; Eve is looking at the tree of knowl-edge. (The Elder and candidate portrays the serpent.)

Serpent   "Yes, hath God said, ye shall not eat of every tree of the garden"?

Eve   "We may eat of the fruit of the trees of the gar-den: But of the fruit of the tree which is in the midst of the garden, God hath said, Ye shall not eat of it, neither shall ye touch it, lest ye die." (Eve added the part neither shall ye touch it)

Serpent   "Ye shall not surely die; for God doth know that in the day ye eat thereof, then your eyes shall be opened, and ye shall be as gods, knowing good and evil."

Eve

(Takes fruit from the tree and eats (may adlib') – shows how yummy it is; then takes a piece to share with Adam. They eat.

Adam

"I have never tasted this fruit before; from which tree did it come?" (Eve points to the tree of knowledge.)

Voice

"Adam! Adam! Adam! (They hid amongst the tree of the garden) "Where art thou?"

Adam

(Comes out of hiding and looks up) "I heard thy voice in the garden, and I was afraid, because I was naked; and I hid myself."

Voice

"Who told thee that thou wast naked?" (Adam looks to Eve and motions her to come out of hiding) "Hast thou eaten of the tree, whereof I commanded thee that thou shouldnst not eat?"

Adam

(Points to Eve) "The woman whom thou gavest to be with me, she gave me of the tree, and I did eat."

Voice

"Woman! What is this that thou hast done?"

Eve

(Looks up – then points to the serpent) "The serpent beguiled me, and I did eat."

Voice

"Because thou hast done this, thou art cursed above all cattle, and above every beast of the field; upon thy belly shalt thou go, (Elder and candidate lie down on their belly) and dust shalt thou eat all the days of thy life: and I will put enmity between thee and the woman, and between thy seed and her seed: it shall bruise thy head, and thou shalt bruise his heel." (Eve looks up) "I will greatly multiply thy sorrow and thy conception; in sorrow thou shalt bring forth children; and thy desire shall be to thy husband, and he shall rule over thee." (Adam looks up) "Because thou hast hearkened unto the voice of thy wife, and hast eaten of the tree, of which I commanded thee, saying, Thou shalt not eat of it; cursed is the ground for thy sake; in sorrow shalt thou eat of it all the days of thy life. Thorns also and thistles shall it bring forth to thee; and thou shalt eat the herb of the field; In the sweat of thy face shalt thou eat bread, till thou return unto the ground; for out of it wast thou taken; for dust thou art, and unto dust shalt thou return."

Adam   (To Eve) "Henceforth, I will not call you woman! Your name is Eve." (Adam and Eve exit).

CHARGE OF LESSON TWO

All brothers (sisters) who received lesson two are seated in chairs in front of the deacons

Stephen   "Brother (Sister) _____ (Names each) What are your thoughts on the lesson you have received?"

Brother/Sister "-------" answers.

Stephen   (Question is repeated until all give their response.) "The dramatization in which you took part is recorded in the Second and Third Chapters of the Book of Genesis of the King James

Version of The Holy Bible. As you portrayed Lucfier in this lesson you are taught to be on guard at all times against this great deceiver. The only way to withstand his temptations is with the power of the Trinity. We receive the power to withstand evil by daily prayer and daily bible reading."

"The sign of this lesson is this (looks up and blinks eyes three times). The blinking of the eyes signifys to us the fall of mankind into sin. As Adam and Eves eyes were opened they became moral...and immoratity was lost"

"The passwords of this lesson are EAT and WOMAN. The passwords are communicated only in the following manner: When a brother (sister) asks, What is this that thou hast done: You answer, EAT. Then you ask, Who gave you of the tree? Your response should be WOMAN." (Seats himself}

Philip

(Stands) ""At the beginning of this lesson Lucifer was cast out of heaven with a third of the host of angels. Because in his heart he wanted to exalt his throne above the star of God. He wanted to be like the Host High. On earth he showed his deceiving ways as he encouraged Eve to partake of the fruit of the forbidden tree in the Garden of Eden. Lucifer is a powerful creation of God --probably the most powerful archangel in heaven. Because of his beauty he wanted to become like God. His name means morning star or angel of light. He can transform himself as he became the beautiful serpent in the Garden of Eden. As a result the serpent received the curse and is as we see the snake today. Satan! The

Devil! Lucifer! The Evil One may disguise evil as something beautiful. From this lesson you see why Adam and Eve were driven from the garden --to till the soil of the earth. The only way for us to defeat the evil ones is with the power we receive from the Trinity. In closing let me read to you (goes and picks up the Bible) from the Book of Revelation. From the twelfth chapter verse nine through verse thirteen. (Reads to them.) This concludes this lesson; you may be seated within the order"

All   "AMEN"

THIRD LESSON RITUAL

The deacons, Elder and secretary take their position in the order.

Stephen   "Honorable Elder?"

Elder   "Yes Brother Stephen/"

Stephen   "Does anyone seek the lessons of our order?"

Elder   "Yes." (Then names the Brother or Sister) _____ Seeks the truth of lesson three.

Stephen   "Bring all brothers (sisters) that seek the truth of lesson three to me."

      Elder goes and returns with those who will receive lesson three. Stands in front of the deacons.

Stephen   (Stands) "Being among us, what do you desire?"

Brother/Sister   "A lesson in truth." (Elder gives the correct an-

41

swer to them.)

Stephen   "Then truth you shall receive; follow your Elder and he will prepare you for lesson three from The Holy Bible." (They Exit room.)

All preparation is made for the ritual: Roles are assigned.

-THE SCENE I-

Elder gives three knocks on the door, then enters. Elder and candidate go and stand center north. Several of the brotherhood is standing around.

Householder   (Enters, looks around, goes to where the brotherhood is standing around.) "Any of ye that will labor for me this day I will pay (They bargin for two dollars a day. May adlib') two dollars. (two or three·'follow him to· the southwest corner.

Householder   (Enters, looks around, goes to where some are standing) "If any of you wish to make wages today, Go to my vineyard and I will pay you what is right at the end of the day! (a couple go any join the others who are working.)

Householder   Repeat as above

Householder   Repeat as above, then he joins the workers.

Elder and candidate joins those standing around.

Householder   (Returns, and sees some standing around. Goes up to the Elder and candidate. "Why stand ye here all the day idle?"

Elder   "Because no man hath hired us?

Householder   "Go ye also into the vineyard; and whatsoever is right, that shall ye receive." (Elder and candidate join the workers.)

(Waits a short time) "Steward! Call the laborers in and pay them."

Steward	"Ye workers! Come form a line to be paid." The Elder and candidate are first in line. They line up in reverse order of hiring. (Pays each $2.00) May adlib' When the ones who were hired first see the two dollars paid to the ones hired last, they think they will receive more. When they are paid $2.00 each goes to the candidate and asks him (her) what he (she) was paid. Everyone except the Elder and candidate protest.
Householder	(Comes to scene when he hears all the loud noise.) "Quiet! Quiet! Please! Quiet! (Noise stops.) "What's the matter?
Laborer	(Points to the Elder and candidate) "They worked only one hour!" (Points to next group) "They worked only three hours!" (Points to next group) "They worked only half the day.) "Thou hast made them all equal unto us which have borne the burden and hear of the day." (The group nod heads in agreement. May adlib').
Householder	"Friend, I do thee no wrong. Didst not thou agree with me to work all day for two dollars?"
Laborer	(Nods head in agreement.)
Householder	(To laborers) "Take that·thine is, and go thy way; I will give unto this last, even as unto thee. Is it not lawful for me to·do what I will with mine own? Is thine eye evil because I am good? So the last shall·be first, and the first last for many be called, but few chosen."

(Elder and candidate exit.)

All preparation is made for Scene II: Role are assigned.

-THE SCENE II-

Elder and candidate enter room, goes to where Stephen is standing.

Elder	(To Stephen) "Good Master, what good things shall I do, that I may have eternal life?"
Stephen	"Why callest thou me good'? (Phase.) "There is none good but one, that is, God: but if thou wilt enter into life, keep the commandments."
Elder	"Which?"
Stephen	Thou shalt do no murder, Thou shalt not commit adultery, Thou shall not steal, Thou shalt not bear false witness, Honour thy father and thy mother: and, Thou shall love thy neighbor as thyself."
Elder	"All these things have I kept from my youth up: What lack I yet?"
Stephen	"If thou wilt be perfect, go and sell that thou hast, and give to the poor, and thou shalt have treasure in heaven: And come and follow me."

(Elder and candidate slowly walk toward exit.)

Stephen	"Verify I say unto you, that a rich man shall hardly enter into the kingdom of heaven."

(Elder and candidate exit. All preparation is made for scene III: Roles are assigned.)

-THE SCENE III-

Elder and candidate enter room and join the two servants standing before the traveler.)

Traveler   "I must journey away for a time. Art! Tom! Traci!. Come." (motions to·servants to come to him. They go to him.) "Arthur, here is five thousand dollars; Be a good steward over·it while I am away." (Art takes money and leaves.)

NOTE: If candidate is a sister,·call Tom second. If candidate is a brother, call Traci second.

"Traci, here is two thousand dollars; be a good steward·over it while I am away." (Traci takes money and leaves) "Tommy, here is one thousand dollars; be a good steward over it while I am away." (The traveler exits room.)

Stephen   (Question is repeated until all give their response.) "The dramatization of the first scene in which you took part is recorded in the twentieth Chapter of the Gospel according to Saint Matthew in The Holy Bible. In your portrail of the laborer who found work late in the day; you received the same reward as the others who had labored longer. There are multiple means to these Scriptures. I strongly encourage each of you to read it often and see the beauty and love of Our Heavenly Father.

In the dramatization of the second scene you portrayed the rich young ruler as recorded in the nineteenth Chapter of the Gospel according to Saint Matthew in The Holy Bible. From this scene our Lord tells you; You must do more than good works and keep the commandments. You! Must do that which he tells you individually ---

and most of all to follow him.

In the dramatization of the third scene you portrayed the servant with one talent as recorded in the Fifth Chapter of the Gospel according to Saint Matthew in The Holy Bible. You did not use that· which was given you; therefor, you lost it and more...

The Sign of this lesson is (takes a coin from his pocket) holding a coin in the right hand eye level and ask: Whose is this image?" (Philip joins Stephen)

Philip   "Caesars." "This is the password."

Stephen   "Render therefor unto Caesar the things that are Caesars --and unto God, the things that are Gods."

Philip   (Goes to The Holy Bible, Picks it up and reads Matthew 6:19-21.) "Lay not up for yourselves treasures upon earth, where moth and rust corrupt, and where thieves break through and steal: But lay up for yourselves treasures in heaven, where neither moth nor rust corrupt, and where thieves do not break through nor steal: For where your treasure is, there your heart be also. This concludes this lesson· you may be seated within the order."'

All   "AMEN"

Traveler   "Go ye unprofitable servant: You are forbidden from my household."

Elder and candidate slowly walk toward the exit. They stop at the deacon blocking their path.

Elder	(To deacon) "Is it lawful to give tribute unto Caesar, or not?"
Deacon I	"Why tempt ye me ye hypocrite! Show me the tribute coin." (Elder give candidate a coin to give to the deacon). Deacon hold the coin up eye level. "Whose is this image and superscription?"
Candidate	(Elder whispers answer to him) "Caesar's."
Deacon I	"Render therefore unto Caesar, the things which are Caesars and, unto God the things that are Gods." (leaves them) Elder and candidate slowly walk toward the exit, they stop at the second deacon who is blocking their path.
Deacon II	"Are you familiar with the story of Ananias and his wife sapphira?"
Candidate	"Yes" or "No"

---If yes then ---

Deacon II	"Tell me what happened? (If the story is correct praise the candidate. At the sign given by the second deacon everyone says "Al-le-lu-la" (The Elder and candidate exit).

---if the answer is incorrect or the answer no –

Deacon II	"To know the story of Ananias and his wife Sapphira Read the first ten verses of the fifth chapter of the Book of Acts in The Holy Bible."

(The Elder and candidate exit).

CHARGE OF LESSON THREE

All brothers (sisters) who received lesson three are seated in chairs in front of the deacons.

Stephen   "Brother (Sister) _____ (names each) What are your thoughts on the lesson you have received?"

Brother/Sister   "--------" answers.

                     The servants with the $5,000 and $2,000 go purchase something from someone in the order: takes what each has purchased to the secretary and sells it to him for twice the price paid for it. (May adlib'}

                     The Elder and candidate go find a spot to hid the $1,000: then they join the other servants.

The traveler returns.

Traveler   "Come! (motions to servant that received $5,000.)"

Arthur   "Thou deliveredst unto me five thousand dollars; Behold, I have gained besides-this five thousand dollars more (gives it to the traveler)."

Traveler   "Well done thou good and faithful servant; Thou has been faithful over a few things: I will make thee ruler over many things! Enter into the joy of my household."

                     "Come! (motions to servant that received $2,000.)"

Traci/Tom   "Thou deliveredst unto me two thousand dollars; Behold, I have gained besides this two thousand dollars more (gives it to the traveler)."

Traveler

"Well done thou good and faithful servant; Thou has been faithful over a few things: I will make thee ruler over many things! Enter into the joy of my·household."

"Come! (motions to servant that received $1,000.)" (Elder and candidate goes and recovers that which they hid, and they return to the traveler.)

Elder

"I knew thee that thou art an hard man, reaping where thou hast not sown, and gathering where thou hast not strawed: I was afraid of losing the one thousand dollars you gave me stewardship over; so I hid thy talent in the earth, lo there thou hast that is thine (hold money toward the traveler.)

Traveler

"You wicked and slothful servant, thou knewest that I reap where I sowed not, and gather where I have not strawed! You could of at least put my money with the exchangers, and there at my coming I would receive my own with usury." (motions to the servant that had two thousand dollars) "Take the thousand dollars from him (her); and give it to him that had stewardship over the ten thousand dollars (take the $1,000 and gives it to the first servant). For unto everyone that hath·shall be given --and he shall have abundance; but, from them that hath not shall be taken away even that which they hath."

FOURTH LESSON RITUAL

The deacons, Elder and secretary take their position in the order.

Stephen	"Honorable Elder?"
Elder	"Yes Brother Stephen."
Stephen	"Does anyone seek the lessons of our order?"
Elder	"Yes." (Then names the Brother or Sister) _____ Seeks the truth of lesson four.
Stephen	"Bring all brothers (Sisters) that seek the truth of lesson four to me."
	Elder goes and returns with those who will receive lesson four. Stands in front of the deacons.
Stephen	(Stands) "Being amoung us, what do you desire?"
Brother/Sister	"A lesson in truth."
Stephen	"Then truth you shall receive; follow your Elder and he will prepare you for lesson four from the Holy Bible." (They exit room.)

All preparation is made for the ritual: Roles are assigned.

-THE SCENE-

Elder and candidate enter. They thresh wheat (may adlib'). The Elder portrays Gideon.

Voice	"And the children of Israel did evil in the sight of the Lord: and the Lord delivered them into the hand of Midian seven years. And the hand of Midian prevailed against Israel; and because of the Midianites the children of Israil made them

the dens which are in the mountains, and caves and strong holds. And so it was, when Israil had sown, that the Midianites came·up, and the A-rnsl-ek-ites, and the children of the east, even they came up against them. And they encamped against them, and destroyed the increase of the earth, till thou come unto Gaza, and left no sustenance for Israel, neither sheep, nor ox, nor ass. For they came up with their cattle and their tents, and they came as grasshoppers for multitude: for both they and their camels were without number; and they entered into the land to destroy it. And Israel was greatly impoverished because of the Midianites; and the children of Israel cried unto the Lord. And it came to pass, when the children of Israel cried unto the Lord because of the Midianites, That the Lord sent a prophet unto the children of Israel, which said unto them, Thus saith the Lord God of Israel, I brought you forth out of the house of bondage; And I delivered you out of the hand of the Egyptians, and out of the hand of all that oppressed you, and drave them out from before you, and gave you their land; And I said unto you, I am the Lord your God; fear not the gods of the Armorites, in whose land ye dwell; but ye have not obeyed my voice."

=Anel (Sats down with his staff and watches them thresh wheat.) Lord walks toward the Angel (Joins the Angel as he approaches Gidean.) "The Lord is with thee, thou mighty man of valour!"

Gideon "Oh my Lord, if the Lord be with us, why then is all this befallen us? And where·be all his miracles which our fathers told us of, saying Did not the Lord bring us up from Egypt/ But now the Lord hath forsaken us, and delivered us unto the hands of the Midianites."

Lord   "Go in this thy might, and thou shalt save Israel from the hand of the Midianites: Have not I sent thee?"

Gideon   "Oh my Lord, wherewith shall I save Israel? Behold, my family is poor in Ma-nas-seh, and I an the least in my father's house."

Lord   "Surely I will be with thee, and thou shalt smite the Medianites as one man."

Gideon   If now I have found grace in thy sight then show me a sign that thou talkest with me. Depart not hence, I pray thee, until I come unto thee, and bring forth my present, and set it before thee."

Lord   "I will tarry until thou come again." (Elder and candidate exit --then return with flesh and unleavened cakes, and broth (artificial fast burning paper and lighter fluid). Presents it to the Lord.

Angel   "Take the flesh and the unleavened cakes, and lay them upon this rock, (fireproff, pan-like top) and pour out the broth over them."

Elder and candidate do as they are told.

Angel   (Puts staff to the rock) Fire consumes all. then leaves.

Gideon   "Alas, O Lord God! For because I have seen an angel of the Lord face to face I shall die (Exodus 33:20).

Lord	"Peace be unto thee; fear not: Thou shalt not die." (Goes out of sight. Elder and candidate built alter unto the Lord.)
Lord	(Approaches Gideon) "Take thy father's young bullock of seven years old, and throw down the altar of Ba-al that thy father hath, and cast down the grove that is by it. Then build an altar unto the Lord thy God upon the top of this rock, in the ordered place, and take the second bullock, and offer a burnt sacrifice with the wood of the grove which thou shalt cut down."
	Lights are dimned. Gideon motions and ten members of the brotherhood join him and the candidate in tearing down altar to Ba-aal, and they cut down the grove. They build altar over rock and offer burnt sacrifice. All return to seats. (Stephen walks by and sees what has happened.)
	Lights are turned up. Several members walk around the destroyed alter to Ba-al (may adlib'). In disbelief each ask the other.
Member	"Who hath done this thing?"
Stephen	(whispers to a member "Gidean."
Member	(Goes and motions rest to come to him) "Gideon the son of Joash hath done this thing!" (they go to where Joash is seated.)
Member	"Joash, Bring out thy son, that he may die; because he hath cast down the altar of Ba-al, and because he halt cut down the grove that was by it."

Joash	(Stands) "Will ye plead for Ba-al? Will ye save him? He that will plead for him, let him be put to death whilst it is yet morning: if he be a god, let him plead for himself, because one hath cast down his altar. Let Ba-al plead against him, because he hath thrown down his altar." (they agree and go to their seats.) Gideon and candidate are alone by altar.
Gideon	(Looks upward prayerful) God, if thou wilt save Israil by mine hand, as thou hast said, Behold I will put a fleece of wool in the floor; and if the dew be on the fleece only, and it be dry upon all the earth beside, then shall I know that thou wilt save Israel by mine hand, as thou hast said (lays down as lights are dimned." Stephen takes spray bottle and wets fleece.) Lights are turned up. (wakes up, goes to the fleece and wringed dew out of the fleece, a bowl full of water). Looks up prayerful. "God, Let not thine anger be hot against me, and I will speak but this once; let me prove, I pray thee, but this once: let me prove, I pray thee, but this once with the fleece; let it now be dry upon all the ground let there be dew.11 (leaves).

Lights are dimned as Stephen takes the spray-bottle and wets the ground, then places fleece on it. Lights turned up. Gideon comes and sees the dry fleece and exits the room.

-THE SCENE II-

Gideon and candidate enter the room; they circle the room clockwise, and all membership of the order join in behind them as a large army. As they walk they sang.

One   On-ward, Christian soldiers. Marching as to war.
       With the cross of Jesus, Going on before!
       Christ to royal Master, Leads a-gainst the foe;
       Forward in-to battle, See His ban-ner go!
       Onward, Christians soldiers, Marching as to war.
       With the cross of Jesus, Going on before!

Two   At the sign of triumph, Satan's host doth flee;
       On then, Christian soldiers, On to victory!
       Hell's foundations quiver. At the shout of praise;
       Brothers, lift your voices, Loud your anthems
       raise!
       On-ward, Christian soldiers, Marching as to war.
       With the cross of Jesus, Going on before!

Three   Like a mighty arrny, Moves the Church of God;
       Brothers, we are treading, where the saints have
       trood;
       We are not divided; All·one body we,
       One in hope and doctrine, One in charity.
       On-ward, Christian soldiers. Marching as to war.
       With the cross of jesus, Going on before!

Four   Onward, then ye people, Join our happy throng,

       Blend with ours your voices, In the triurnph
       song;
       Glory, land and honor, Un-to Christ the King;
       This thro countless ages, Men and angels sing.
       On-ward, Christian soldiers. Marching as to war.
       With the cross of Jesus, Going on before!

Lord   (Approaches Gideon) "The people that are with
       thee are too many for me to give the Midian-
       ites into their hands, lest Israel vaunt themselves
       against me saying, mine own hand hath saved
       me. Proclaim to the people this (whispers to

Gideon)."

Gideon (Makes another half circle with the people following then stops) "Whosoever is fearful and afraid let him return to his home!"

Several "Al-le-lu-la" (may adlib') What's what I wanted to hear." (others) "That's good preaching!" (several return to their seats.)

Gideon makes another circle with the people following, They sang stanza three.

Lord (approaches Gideon) "The people are yet too many: bring them down unto the water, and I will try them for thee there, and it shall be, that of whom I say unto thee, this shall go with thee, and the same shall gom with thee; and of whomsoever I say unto thee; This shall not go with thee, the same shall not go."

Stephen "Why can't I just go get the Midianites? Lets forget Dads altar to Baal."

Philip "No! First, things have to be set right in thy household."

Stephen "Well, If I have to tear that altar down, do you care if I do it at night?"

Philip "Makes no difference the time you do it; just do it!" (To the ones who received the lesson) "You know, I believe the Lord had been working on Joash too; and he was happy that Gidion had torn down that altar. He showed wisdom in saving Gideon's life. The Bible says the spirit of the Lord came upon Gideon, and he blew a trumpet --That was the sweetest sound the Israel Nation had heard in years and thirty-three thousand answered the call to fight. The only thing wrong was that two hundred thousand Midianites show up."

Stephen   "I need more confirmation from the Lord."

Philip   "Our Lord shows extreme patiences. As he answered the fleeces of Gideon, He will answer our fleeces today, when we need confirmation; yet, He wants us to grow. If ·we spend our lives putting out fleeces, sooner or later we are the one who gets fleeced. Then the Lord told Gideon he had too many men."

Stephen   "What do you mean I have too many men? Look at all those Midianites!"

Philip   "Yes, you have too many men for me to give the Midianites unto their hands; lest Israel will say they saved themselves Tell all that are fearful and afraid to go home."

Stephen   "Lord, I told them and twenty-three thousand left me --I have only ten thousand men left."

Philip   "You still have too many men."

Stephen   "WHAT!"

Philip   "Take the men down to the water and lets watch them drink."

Stephen   "You guys go to the river and get a drink --and please be careful how you drink."

Philip   "That's your army --the ones who put their hand to their mouth to drink!"

Stephen	"No, Lord! Give me the ones that lappeth as a dog."
Philip	"No. That's your army."
Stephen	"But here is only three hundred."

Philip returns to his seat.

"Gideon tells them to do as he does, blow their trumpets when he blows his trumpet; to break their pitcher when he breaks his; to hold their lamps in their left hand and to stand still as he does. Each did as he was told and the Midianites were defeated as by one man. Some of those who were send home would probably would have blowed their trumpet when he wanted to. Not when directed to; and some would have said, I'm not going to break my pitcher --that's my wifes best pitcher! She'd kill me if I break her pitcher. But the three hundred performed as one; as the Lord had said."

"The sign of this lesson is the left hand up as holding a lamp (makes sign).

The password of this lesson is Jehovah-Sha-lorn. That is the name given the altar Gideon built. The password is communicated in the following manner (Philip joins Stephen).

Philip	"There is an altar in Oph'-rah of the A'-bi-ez'-rites."
Stephen	"What is its name?"
Philip	"Jehovah-Sha-lom. Who built this altar?"
Stephen	"Gideon. This concludes this lesson. You may be

seated within the order."

All   "AMEN"

(Lord walks with Gideon and followers as they make half circle sanging stanza four.)

Gideon   (Hold up hand to stop) "Go to the water and drink!" (All followers began to drink.)

Lord (To Gideon) "Every one that lappeth of the water with his tongue as a dog lappeth water send home, And the number of them that lapped, putting their hand to their mouth will be your army that I will save and deliver to the Nidianites into thine hand." (The Lord leaves

Gideon   (Goes to the ones lapping the water like a dog) "Go home." (just three are left; they lay to rest.)

Lord (Approaches Gideon)   "Arise, get thee down unto the host; for I have delivered it unto thine hand. But if thou fear to go down, go thou with Phurah, thy servant, down to the host. And thou shalt hear what they say and you will be strengthened) Exits.

Gideon   (Takes candidate only; they go to where the door is part open and listen.)

1st Voice   "Behold, i dreamed a dream, and, lo a'cake of barley bread tumbled into the host of Midian, and came unto a tent, and destroyed it.:

2nd Voice   "This is nothing else save the sword of Gideon, the son of Joash, a man of Israel: for unto his hand hath God delivered Midian, and all the host."

Gideon	"Al-le-lu-la!" (kneels and prays. They return to the army) "Arise; for the Lord hath delivered unto your hand the host of Midean." (He divides them into three groups) "Look on me, and do likewise; and behold, when i come to the outside of the camp, it shall be that, as I do, so shall ye do. When i blow with a trumpet, I and all that are with me, then blow ye the trumpts song say, The sword of the Lord and of Gideon." (all exit)
Outside	You can hear the trumpet blo
	You can hear "The sword of the Lord and of Gidean"
	You can hear glass breaking
	Stomping of feet. (All return to the room and are seated.)

CHARGE OF LESSON FOUR

All brothers (sisters) who received lesson four are seated in chairs in front of the deacons.

Stephen	"Brother (Sister) (names each) What are your thoughts on the lesson you have received?"
Brother/Sister	"-------" answers.

Question is repeated until all give their responses.

Stephen	(Stands) "The dramatization inwhich you took part is recorded in the Sixth and Seventh Chapters of the Book of Judges in the Old Testaments of The Holy Bible. As you portrayed Gideon in this lesson we discover many truths.

When the Angel of the Lord first spoke to you,I think it shows maybe a sense of humor with our God. You were trying to save a little wheat for yourself, hiding from the Midianites, when the Angel said, The Lord is with thee, Thou mighty man of Valour! At this point thou your family is poor and you are least in your fathers house; you ask two very good questions. First, If the Lord is with us why are all these Midianites taking our livelyhood? and, Second, Where are all the miracles that our fathers have told us you proform? The answer to both these questions are the same: They did evil in the sight of the Lord. Only when the children of Israel cried unto the Lord because of the Midianites did the Lord send a prophet. You know Gideon wasn't much different than we today --his first request is show me a sign! Have you ever asked for a sign? The fire consumed his offering and he's ready to go get the Midianites; but the Lord says wait! I can see Gideon now; all fired up knowing he has been chosen after seeing the sign, not wanting to wait. The dialogue could have been:

(Philip joins Stephen)

Philip   "Wait!"

Stephen "Don't have time to wait Lord --let me go get those Midianites!"

Philip   "There's something I want you to do before I deliver the Midianite unto you."

Stephen "What's that Lord? There's nothing more important!"

Philip   "First, you know the altar to Baal that's at your

home?"

Stephen	"Yea, Dad's very proud of that altar."
Philip	"Well, I want you to tear it down and cut down that grove beside it."

FIFTH LESSON RITUAL

The deacons, Elder and Secretary take their position in the order.

Stephen	"Honorable Elder?"
Elder	"Yes Brother Stephen."
Stephen	"Does anyone seek the lessons of our order?"
Elder	"Yes. Brother (sister) _____ seeks the truth of lesson five."
Stephen	"Bring all brothers (sisters) that seek the truth of lesson five to me."

Elder goes and returns with those who will receive lesson five. They stand in front of the deacons.

Stephen	"(stands) "Being among us, what do you desire?"
Brother Sister	"A lesson in truth."
Stephen	"Then truth you shall receive: Follow your Elder and he will prepare you for lesson five from The Holy Bible." (They exit room.)

PART ONE

-THE SCENE I-

Elder and candidate enter, join others at center of room. Watches as father carrys money to bank (secretary desk}. The Elder portrays the son.

Son   (Elder and candidate approach the father) "Father, give me the portion of goods that falleth to me."

Father   "Today, I will give thee thy portion" (Goes to bank, gets large stack of money and returns. At a table he divides the money into two equal stacks. Gives one stack of money to a servant who·returns it to the bank. Speaks to another servant. "Go ask my sons to come to me."

Servant   (Goes to each son) "Your father desires your presence."

Sons   (Each goes to their father) "You sent for me?"

Father   "Yes." (Divides the money into two stacks. In one stack he puts two bills for each bill he puts in the other stack. Give the older son the larger stack.) "Take thy portion." (Gives the younger son, candidate, the small stack of money.) "Take thy portion." The younger son puts his money in a box and goes back to where he was when the servant called him. The older son takes his money to the bank. The Elder and candidate take the box of money they have and exits the room.

-THE SCENE II-

Five stations have been set up for this scene. (Elder and candidate enter and go to the first station.)

First Station   (Barroom music if available.) Adlibs. Motions several to join them as the candidate buys drinks for all.

Elder and candidate goes to second station. Others follow.

Second Station   (Sats at table and eats.) Adlibs. Pays the bill for all. They all leave and go toward the third station.

On way to the third station a peddler comes to the candidate and sell him a piece of paper that says on it Brooklyn Bridge.

Third Station   (Buys cars of himself and friends.) Adlibs.

Fourth Station   (Gives girls money.) Adlibs.

Fifth Station   (Sats with friends at a table and orders drinks.) Candidate counts his mones. Adlibs. Motions to friends that he can only pay for himself. All friends leave. Gives ring off his hand to settle bar bill and leaves.

Elder and candidate make circle of room; pleads with all he has encountered before (they all shake their heads no or stick their nose in the air to avoid him.)

Meets a person with water. Gives the person his pair of shoes off his feet for a drink.

Finally, Elder and candidate meet a person and agrees with everything the person says (Adlibs). They go into field and feed swine. Dim lights for one minute. When lights are turned up the face of the Elder lights up (he has an ideal!).

Elder   "How many hired servants of my father's have bread enough and to spare, and I perish with hunger!" (Goes with candidate to the person he works for and quits.)

"I will go to my father, and will say unto him, Father, I have sinned against heaven, and before thee --and am no more worthy to be called thy son. Make me as one of thy hired servants." (Exits room.)

-THE SCENE III-

(Elder and candidate enter the room.)

Father (Sees son enter. Runs to him and hugs him)

"You're alive!"

Son "Father, I have sinned against heaven and in thy sight, and am no more worthy to be called thy son."

Father (Thankful shakes sone hand looking him over.)

(To servant who has joined them) "Bring forth the best robe and put it on him; and put a ring on his hand, and shoes on his feet!"

Servant (Returns with purple robe and puts it on son: Places ring on his finger, puts shoes on his feet.)

Father "And bring hither the fatted calf, and kill it, and let us eat and make merry. For this my son was dead and is alive again; he was lost, and is found." (Exits room. Merry music is heard from outside the door.)

PART TWO

-THE SCENE IV-

Elder and candidate now portray the eldest son. Room is dimned, the Elder and candidate enter and go to the east side. Lights are turned up. They hear the merry music from outside the room an walk toward it.

Son	(See a servant and motions him to come.) "What's going on inside?"
Servant	(Happy) "Thy brother is come; and thy father hath killed the fatted calf, because he hath received him safe and sound." (Exits)
Son	(Acts mad. Sats down and pouts.)
Father	(Comes into room and goes to son.) "Come rejoice with us, your brother is safe and at home."
Son	"Lo these many years, do I serve thee, neither transgressed I at any time thy commandment; And yet thou never gavest·me a kid; that I might make merry with my friends. But as soon as this thy son! was come, which hath devoured thy living with harlots, thou hast killed for him the fatted calf!"
Father	(Puts arm around him.) "Son, thou are ever with me, and all that I have is thine. It was meet that we should make merry, and be glad; for this thy brother was dead, and is alive again; and was lost, and is found." (All exit room).

-CHARGE OF LESSON FIVE-

All brothers (Sisters) who received lesson five are seated in chairs in front of the deacons.

Stephen   "Brother (Sister) _____ (names each), what are your thoughts on the lesson you have received?"

Brother
Sister   "--------". Answers.

Question is repeated until all give their responses.

Stephen   (Stands) "The dramatization in which you took part is recorded in the fifteenth chapter of the Gospel according to Saint Luke in the King James Version of The Holy Bible. In the first part you portrayed the youngest prodigal son, both were prodigal! For you to understand the young son we have divided his story into six parts: RENEWAL! REBELLION! RECKONING! REALIZATION! REPENTANCE! and RESTORATION! All begin with the letter "R". (Sats down unless he is to give more of charge.)

     (NOTE: Stephen may give the complete charge or it may be divided as you see fit.)

Nicotas   (Stands) "It's clear a man had two sons. We will never know the difference in their ages. I suspect there was very little difference; maybe, a year or two. During their youth and teen years the brothers could have been very close to one another --then as manhood was reached it's possible the older brother aided in the awareness of his younger brother that they were sons and heirs of a very wealthy father and influenced his brother to ask for the portion of goods that falleth to him because, he knew his father would divide with both of them. After their father gave them of their inheritance; it's possible the older brother caused the young son to leave. I can hear him bossing his young brother and telling him, if you don't like me telling you what to do --then why don't you leave? The Bible says: And not many·days after the younger son gathered all together, and took his journey into a far country." (Sats down)

Second he realizes he has to share this inheritance. Greed, hate, selfishness and everything else sets in. (Sats down.)

Parmenas

(Stands) "The rebellion of the eldest son can be seen in his greed, hate, lying, selfishness and other hang-ups. Two times in this story we see his rebellion: The Bible says, Now his elder son was in the field, and as he came and drew near the house he heard music and dancing. Remember, this was the eldest son of a wealthy man; there was no reason for him to be in the field; unless, he had done some riotous living of his own. Could it be possible he had lost all his money too, and had had to move back into his fathers house, where he was an overseer? He could easily blame his younger brother for all that had happened to him.

If my younger brother hadn't asked for that portion that falleth us I would still have mine:

If my father had given only my younger his portion I would still have mine. If! If! If! (sats down)

Timon

(Stands) "He called one of the servants and asked what going on in the house. It must have hit him like a sledge hammer when the servant said; thy brother is come! His day of reckoning was at hand. After having told everyone that his brother was dead --now he shows up. The servant that told him that his brother had come; had waited for this day. I suspect this was an elder servant that had been with the father a long time; was there when the boys were born; he had seen them grow up and go their seperate ways --yet so much alike. He was very loyal and loving toward his master. He probably told the son when he come from the field and asked what was going on. You know thy brother which you told your father was dead, well he's home! And he was angry, and would not go in. If things had been right between him and his father there would have been no need to call a servant to find out what was going on. He would have rejoiced with his father that his brother was home. Reckoning comes to us Christians too. Don't we sometimes find it hard to rejoice with other Christians when something good happens to them. How hard it is for a childless couple who wants a baby to attend a christening --Or attend the party of a fellow worker who received the promation you felt you deserved and were going to get. It is far easier to weep with those who weep than to rejoice then there is rejoicement." (Sats down)

Nicanor

(Stands) "Therefore "Therefore come his father out. Again, we see the love of the father is the same for both sons. If the younger son hadn't returned these two may have never been reconciled. The act of his no good brothers return brings out all that is being held inside him. Lo, these many years do I serve thee; neither trangressed I at any time thy commandment, and yet thou never gavest ne a kid that I might make merry with my friends. Hear the legalism. It's just not fair! I can hear him say. Well let me tell you my friends: When the Lord wants to deal with you and bring some things to light, you'll be surprised at how many things may seem unfair. The older son has his me, my, mine, I, I, I. But as soon as this thy son was come, which hath devoued thy living with harlots; thou hast killed for him the fatted calf. Notice he says thy son; not my brother. And which devoured thy living. Be spent only the inheritance that was freely given him. The older brother had no way of knowing how the money was spent, but we see how he would have spent the money in a far country on wine, women and song. To make matters worse the calf was probably his pet. The older son realizes he has brought all this on himself." {Sats down)

Prochorus (Stands) "And he said unto him. Son, thou art ever with me, and all that I have is thine. The father stands there and takes all this abuse from the eldest son. And after this son gets it all out, when all the resentment and hate of years all come to light the father does the same with him as he did with his younger brother. Remember when the young son confessed to his father that the father was so happy that he wouldn't let him complete his repentance, but starts ordering for a celebration." (Sats down)

Philip   (Stands) "It was meet that we should make merry, and be glad; for this thy brother was dead, and is alive again, and was lost and is found. We don't know how long the father and older son were outside, I like to think that everything surfaced from this prodigal. I can see the heart warming picture as the father put his arm around this eldest son and they go inside together. How the brothers rejoice at seeing each other. How the young brother tells what has happened to him in his life to his older brother, and the older brother tells his younger brother all that has happen to him. The joy in this household as all are reconciled." (Sats down)

Stephen   (Stands) "The sign of this lesson is (gives sign) the right hand extended to receive money, as the prodigal sons did when receiving their inheritance. The passwords of this lesson are Renewal, Rebellion, Reckoning, Realization, Repentance and Restoration. The passwords are communicated only in the following manner. (Philip joins Stephen)

Parrnenas   (Stands) "The young son went into rebellion! The drift between the two sons could have developed during this time. In his rebellion the young son took that which was his and journied to a far country. He probably left mad; maybe, even told them all he never wanted to see any of them again in his anger. At this time I would like to make a point about us Christians being in a far country --: believe any time we get outside the will of God or do our own thing without Divine Guidance --then we are in a far country!"

All   "AMEN!"

Parmenas

"In this far country we are told this prodigal son wasted his substance with riotous living. Again, we can only guess at the number of years it took him to go broke. I suggest he was in rebellion for a long period. You know the Lord has a way of working circumstances for each of us. --they're taylor-rnade to deal with things in our lives that the Lord wants brought to the surface and for us to deal with. He has one set of circumstances for me, and another set for you; or, he may use the same set to deal with the both of us." (Sats down)

Timon

(Stands) "And he went and joined himself to a citizen of that country; and he sent him into his fields to feed swine. After this prodigal son looses everything he begans to reckon with himself, on what has happen to him. He discoverys everything has went downhill since he left his fathers authority:

He had no one who loved him!

He had no one who had his best interest at heart!

He had no one to give him guidance!

In reckoning with himself he realized he needed to be under authority; so he attaches himself to a citizen. We don't know how long he was under the authority of this citizen; but, during this time he becomes aware of his circumstance --of what had happened to his life: Why it had happen: And that no one was to be blamed except himself." (Sats down)

Nicanor

(Stands) "And he would fain have filled his belly with the husks that the swine did eat; and no man gave unto him. He's learning the facts of life the hard way --his own experience. He learns only he is in charge of his destiny. He comes to himself and said; How many hired servants of my fathers have bread enough and to spare and I perish with hunger! Realization comes to him that he is still his fathers son. I will arise and go to my father: Notice he says my father; I suspect he wrote him off as a dumb O'Dad when he left home. I will say unto him; Father I have sinned against heaven, and before thee, and am no more worthy to be called thy son, make me as one of your hired servants. When he had left home everything had been me! me! me! my! mine! I! I! I! He returns home just wanting to serve. (Sats down.)"

Prochorus   (Stands) "But when he was yet a great way off, his father saw him, and had compassion, and ran and fell on his neck and kissed him. And the son said unto him: Father, I have sinned against heaven and in thy sight, and am no more worthy to be called thy son. The repentance of the son is said to the father. Do you suspect there might have been a moment of doubt as he saw his father running to greet him? Seeing his O'Man rush toward him it would have been easy for him to just let his father welcome him home; and to enjoy the benefits of the household. We have to admire this young prodigal: He did exactly as he said he was going to do. Father, I have sinned against heaven and in thy sight, and am no mor worthy to be called thy son. His father doesn't let him finish." (Sats down)

Philip   (Stands) "Bring forth the best robe, and put it on him, and put a ring on his hand, and shoes on his feet, and bring hither the fatted calf, and kill it. And let us eat and be merry: For this my son was dead and is alive again; he was lost and is found!

Here I would like to mention some facts concerning the father: First, the father didn't have to divide or give the sons their inheritance when it was asked. He could have said no, you're too young to know how to manage your inheritance; but he gave a portion of their inheritance to them. We Christians have an inheritance today, and I think Our Heavenly Father wants us to claim it. The father didn't tell the boys that if they didn't listen to him that he would take it back. He gave to them freely to use wisely or to misuse --no strings attached. Our Lord freely give to us of our inheritance; and, the only way we can keep from misusing it is to stay close to his guidance. The Bible says, but when he was yet a great way off; his father saw him. All the time he had been gone his father had continuely watched for his return ---when he would come to his senses and return home. I suspect the father had even told his servants, to keep watch for the son to return. There was really no need for anyone to watch because I suspect the older son had told all that he had received word that his brother had died. He had compassion, and ran and fell on his neck, and kissed him. Needless, to say, the love of the father is overwhelming. Should any of you Samaritans be called on for a devotion, lesson or talk: Use this lesson, and use the title: The Day God Ran."

(sats down)

Nicotas   (Stands) "In the first part of this lesson we see the six phases of the young prodigal son who strayed: In the last part of this lesson we see the same six phases apply to the older prodigal son who stayed. In the first place being older; the eldest son became aware first that they were the sons of a wealthy man.

Philip   "Have you read the story of the prodigal sons?"

Stephen   "Yes, there are six phases in each ones life."

Philip   "Name the six phases." (Sats down)

Stephen   "Renewal, Rebellion, Reckoning, Realization, Repentance, Restoration."

"There is a grand hailing sign for this lesson. It is given like this (gives sign); hold arms and hands extended, extend the four fingers and thumb on the right hand, extend only the finger nest to the thumb on the left hand. This number is for the six R's. This concludes this lesson. You may be seated within the order."

All   "AMEN!"

Chapter 6

Do you have a favorable opinion of the Samaritan Order?

Do you think the lessons in the order can be applied to your life?

Do you know, beyond doubt, that when you die you will spend eternity with Jesus?

If not make your commitment to Jesus today!

Without Jesus you are separated from God and without hope of eternal life.

To obtain eternal life is easy. First, you need to be saved. "For all have sinned and come short of the glory of God." (Romans 3:23) "I tell you, Nay: but, except ye repent, ye shall all likewise perish." (Luke 13:3) Second, you cannot save yourself. "Not by works of righteousness which we have done, but according to His mercy He saved us." (Titus 3:5) Third, Jesus has provided for your salvation. "For God so loved the world that He gave His only begotten Son that whosoever believeth in Him should not perish but have everlasting life." (John 3:16) Fourth, you must accept Jesus for salvation. (salvation is free! But, following Jesus is not free). "Believe in the Lord Jesus Christ, and thou shalt be saved." (Acts 16:31) Fifth, now is the time to accept Jesus as savior.

"Behold, now is the day of salvation." (11 Cor:6.2) What to do. "That if thou shalt confess with thy mouth the Lord Jesus, and shalt believe in thine heart that God hath raised Him from the dead, thou shalt be saved." (Romans 10:9) Finally, will you bow your head and pray this prayer! I know that I am a sinner, and am headed for Hell. I am willing to turn from the sin in my life and make You the Lord and Master of my life. Forgive all my sins and come into my heart right now and save me. For I pray in Jesus Christ's name. Amen.

Do you remember in the petition for membership in the Samaritan order "Is it your desire to become a disciple of Jesus, Our Lord, Son of the Most High, and serve the Trinity? Only Christians are eligible to become members. The name Samaritan was chosen because it tells of our willingness to serve, and to love all.

In the story of the good Samaritan, Christ illustrated the nature of true religion. He shows that it consists not in systems, creeds, or rites, but in the performance of loving deeds, in bringing the greatest good to others, in genuine goodness.

As Jesus was teaching the people, "a certain lawyer stood up and tempted Him, saying, Master, what shall I do to inherit eternal life?" With breathless attention the large congregation awaited the answer. The priests and rabbis had thought to entangle Jesus by having the lawyer ask this question. But Jesus entered into no controversy. Jesus required the answer from the questioner himself. "What is written in the law?" He said " how readest thou?" The Jews still accused Jesus of lightly regarding the law given from Sinai; but He turned the question of salvation upon the keeping of God's commandments.

The lawyer said, "Thou shalt love the Lord thy God with all thy heart, and with all thy soul, and with all thy strength, and with all thy mind; and thy neighbor as thyself." Jesus said, "Thou hast answered right: This do, and thou shalt live."

The lawyer was not satisfied with the position and works of the Pharisees. He had been studying the Scriptures with a desire to learn their real meaning. He had a vital interest in the matter, and had asked their real meaning in all sincerity. "What shall I do?" In his answer as to the requirements of the law, he passed by all the ceremonial and ritualistic precepts. For those he claimed no value, but presented the two great principles on which hang all the law and the prophets. This answer, being commended by Christ, placed the Saviour on vantage ground with the rabbis. They could not condemn Him for sanctioning that which had been advanced by an expositor of the law.

"This do, and thou shalt live," Jesus said. He presented the law as a divine unity, and in this lesson taught that it is not possible to keep one precept and break another; for the same principle runs through them all. Man's destiny will be determined by his obedience to the whole law. Supreme love to God and impartial love to man are the principles to be wrought out in the life.

The lawyer found himself a lawbreaker. He was convicted under Jesus's searching words. The righteousness of the law, which he claimed to understand, he had not practiced. He had not manifested love toward his fellow man. Repentance was demanded; but instead of repenting he tried to justify himself. Rather than acknowledge the truth, he sought to show how difficult of fulfillment the commandment is. Thus he hoped both to parry conviction and to vindicate himself in the eyes of the people. Jesus words had shown that his question was needless, since he had been able to answer it himself. Yet he put another question, saying, "Who is my neighbor?"

Among the Jews this question caused endless dispute. They had no doubt as to the heathen and the Samaritans; these were strangers and enemies. But where should the distinction be made amount the people of their own nation, and among the different classes of society? Whom should the priest, the rabbi, the elder, regard as neighbor? They spent their lives in a round of ceremonies to make themselves pure. Contact with the ignorant and careless multitude, they taught, would cause denounce the bigotry of those who were watching to condemn Him. But by a simple story He held up before His hearers such a picture of the outflowing of heaven-born love as touched all hearts, and drew from the lawyer a confession of the truth.

The way to dispel darkness is to admit light. The best way to deal with error is to present truth. It is the revelation of God's love that makes manifest the deformity and sin of the heart centered in self.

"A certain man," said Jesus, "was going down from Jerusalem to Jericho; and he fell among robbers, which both Stripped him and eat him, and departed, leaving him half dead. And by chance a certain priest was going down that way; and when he saw him he passed by on the other side. And in like manner a Levite also, when he came to the place, and saw him, passed by on the other side. "This was no imaginary scene, but an actual occurrence. In journeying from Jerusalem to Jericho, the traveler had to pass through a portion of the wilderness of Judea. The road led down a wild, rocky ravine, which was infested by robbers, and was often the scene of violence. It was here that the traveler was attacked, stripped of all that was valuable, wounded and bruised, and left half dead by the wayside. As he lay thus, the priest came that way but he merely glanced toward the wounded man. Then the Levite appeared. Curious to know what had happened, he stopped and looked at the sufferer. He wished that he had not come that way, so that he need not have seen the wounded man. He persuaded himself that the case was no concern of his.

Both these men were in sacred office, and professed to expound the Scriptures. They were of the class specially chosen to be representatives of God to the people. They were to "have compassion on the ignorant, and on them that are out of the way", that they might lead men to understand God's great love toward humanity.

The angels of heaven look upon the distress of God's family upon the earth, and they are prepared to co-operate with men in relieving oppression and suffering. God in His providence had brought the priest and the Levite along the road where the wounded sufferer lay, that they might see his need of mercy and help. All heaven watched to see if the hearts of these men would be touched, with pity for human woe. Jesus had instructed the Hebrews in the wilderness; from the pillar of cloud and of fire He had taught a very different lesson from that which the people were now receiving from their priest and teachers. The merciful provisions of the law extended even to the lower animals, which cannot express in words their want and sufferings.

Directions had been given to Moses for the children; of Israel to this effect: "If thou meet thine enemy's ox or his ass going astray, thou shalt surely bring it back to him. If thou see the ass of him that hateth thee lying under his burden, and wouldest forbear to help him, thou shalt surely help with him" (Ex. 23:4,5). But in the man wounded by robbers, Jesus presented the case of a brother in suffering. How much more should their hearts have been moved with pity for him than a beast of burden! The message had been given them through Moses that the Lord their God, "a great God, a mighty, and a terrible," "doth excute the judgment of the fatherless and widows, and loveth the stranger." Wherefore He commanded, "Love ye therefore the stranger."

"Thou shalt love him as thyself." With all these lessons the priest and the Levite were familiar, but they had not brought them into practical life. In their action, as Jesus had described it, the lawyer saw nothing contrary to what he had been taught concerning the requirement of the law. But now another scene was presented.

A certain Samaritan, in his journey, came where the sufferer was, and when he saw him, he had compassion on him. He did not question whether the stranger was a Jew or a Gentile. If a Jew, the Samaritan well knew that, were their condition reversed, the man would spit in his face, and pass him by with contempt. But he did not hesitate on account of this. He did not consider that he himself might be in danger of violence by tarrying in the place. It was enough that there was before him a human being in need and suffering. He took off his own garment with which to cover him. The oil and wine provided for bis own journey was used to heal and refresh the wounded man. He lifted him on his own beast, And carried him to a nearby inn. For several days he looked after the mans needs; then when he had to leave to left a sum of money and told the innkeeper, to care after the mans needs. And if more payment was needed he would pay it on his return trip.

Johnson became my friend, we did several more weeks of working and talking together, with me supplying his breakfast and lunch each day, then he would ride off on his bike to return the next day. I looked forward to our discussions each day ----for he had an insight to some of our bible discussions that I had never thought of in the way he explained it.

Chapter 7

By now I knew that Johnson was homeless, and while we were the same size I gave him some of my clothes. A strange thing; his clothes were always clean now, not like the first day we met him. One morning Johnson told me he was going to a new job and would not be available to work with me. We had never talked, or me ask him questions about his family. I ask how I could get in touch with h.im when I had more work. His reply was "you can't"! There is no way. I ask where his family lived. He seemed puzzled at this question, then I ask if his father and mother were alive. Again he didn't answer. So, I used a trick I had used many times in my salesman years: To ask a question, then remain silent. I ask where did you attend school? It was quiet for minutes, that seems like hours --but I stood my ground and said nothing. "Ted", he finally said. "I don't remember my childhood, perhaps I was raised in an orphanage, I've never had any family or schooling." With hast he got on his bike and left. I didn't know what to do. I owed him several days wages, and now he was gone. With no way to get in touch with him, I finished the work in my yard. I sure did miss Johnson..... And prayed he would be safe and healthy – wherever he was.

Years have now passed, since my encounter with Johnson, seldom do I think of him anymore. My wife of thirty-five years has died, and I have remarried to a beautiful Christian lady, her husband had died a few years before my wife, Faye. As we age more people who meet us think we have been married a very long time. When we are asked how we met we tell them we met in prison, joking. The year after Faye died I rededicated my life to Christ. I spent my time mostly at Ceta Canyon, our Methodist Camp, was president of the Methodist men at Lakeridge Methodist Church, and went on the "The walk to Emmaus", a weekend spiritual encounter to learn how the serve the church and Christ more fully. Within this organization was the prison ministry called "Karios". That is where I met my wife, Corky. We became very active in the Walk to Emmaus and Karios; As a matter of face: We served on the national team of Walk to Emmaus that went to Sweden to begin the walk there. On this trip we had a wonderful time... After the walk finished in Sweden ended, Corky and I spent time in Paris and London.

I still think of Johnson from time to time. I remember the story he told me how a deck of cards was his Bible. Later he told me in the deck of cards was two Jokers: These Jokers represented the two choices we each must make in our life. We can repent of our sins, ask Jesus to come into our life and live for Him and have our name written in the "Lambs book of life" --Or stay a sinner and spend eternity in Hell --WHAT IS YOUR CHOICE?

Johnson and I discussed many things while we worked together. Once he ask me if I could name the twelve disciples. They are Simon (called Peter), Andrew, James (the son of Zehades), John, Philip, Barthomew, Thomas, Matthew, James (the son of Alopha), Thaddaus, Simon, and Judas. He questioned me on who I thought was the greatest Prophet? Was it bIsaiah? Jeremiah? Ezekiel? Or one of the others?

We also discussed some of the women in the Bible too. Naomi and Ruth, and the Samaritan woman at the well where Jesus asked for drink of water; then the was Ester, who saved her people, and don't forget Herodias (who caused the death of John the Baptist). !

Chapter 8

Like I said at the start of Chapter 1: "Johnson was no ordinary angel!" He knew the Bible inside-out. The only thing I ask him he didn't know was the first thing when we landed on the moon "What was the first thing Neil Armstrong and fellow astronauts did? They took communion (the last supper) I could tell Johnson got disgusted when we would talk about what we Christian here on earth knew about the Bible. He said a very few knew what the "Beatitudes" are --or where to find them in the Bible; and the "Transfiguration" would bring a puzzle look. He was surprised in my answer when ask to name some parables: Mustard seed, Great feast, Two sons, Evil farmer, Vineyard workers, Unforgiving debtor; Lost sheep, Hidden treasure, Wheat and weeds, Farmer scattering seed, Three servants, and Ten brides-maids (there's others I couldn't recall at the time).

The one thing all knew was the "Resurrection".

I do hope you have enjoyed reading this book! Parts of it was wrote over forty years ago.

Recently I have written several other books: *My Look At the Bible, Between The Lines a book of Short Stories* and publish a Quarterly Magazine "From The Cross".

May God Bless each of you!